Dear Parents and Educators,

Welcome to Penguin Young Readers! As parents and educators, you know that each child develops at his or her own pace—in terms of speech, critical thinking, and, of course, reading. Penguin Young Readers recognizes this fact. As a result, each Penguin Young Readers book is assigned a traditional easy-to-read level (1–4) as well as a Guided Reading Level (A–P). Both of these systems will help you choose the right book for your child. Please refer to the back of each book for specific leveling information. Penguin Young Readers features esteemed authors and illustrators, stories about favorite characters, fascinating nonfiction, and more!

Dick and Jane: Who Can Help?

LEVEL **2**

GUIDED READING LEVEL **E**

This book is perfect for a **Progressing Reader** who:
- can figure out unknown words by using picture and context clues;
- can recognize beginning, middle, and ending sounds;
- can make and confirm predictions about what will happen in the text; and
- can distinguish between fiction and nonfiction.

Here are some **activities** you can do during and after reading this book:
- Read the Pictures: Use the pictures in this book to tell the story. Go through the book, retelling the story just by looking at the pictures.
- Titles: The title of a story is very important. It should catch the reader's attention and say something about the story. Each of the seven stories in this book has a title. Come up with a new title for each story.

Remember, sharing the love of reading with a child is the best gift you can give!

—Bonnie Bader, EdM
    Penguin Young Readers program

*Penguin Young Readers are leveled by independent reviewers applying the standards developed by Irene Fountas and Gay Su Pinnell in *Matching Books to Readers: Using Leveled Books in Guided Reading*, Heinemann, 1999.

PENGUIN YOUNG READERS
Published by the Penguin Group
Penguin Group (USA) LLC, 375 Hudson Street, New York, New York 10014, USA

USA | Canada | UK | Ireland | Australia | New Zealand | India | South Africa | China
penguin.com
A Penguin Random House Company

Dick and Jane is a registered trademark of Addison-Wesley Educational Publishers, Inc. From GUESS WHO. Copyright © 1951 by Scott, Foresman and Company, copyright renewed 1979. From THE NEW WE COME AND GO. Copyright © 1956 by Scott, Foresman and Company, copyright renewed 1984. All rights reserved. First published in 2004 by Grosset & Dunlap, an imprint of Penguin Group (USA) Inc. Published in 2012 by Penguin Young Readers, an imprint of Penguin Group (USA) Inc., 345 Hudson Street, New York, New York 10014. Manufactured in China.

Library of Congress Control Number: 2003016828

ISBN 978-0-448-43407-0

PENGUIN YOUNG READERS

LEVEL
PROGRESSING
READER
2

Dick and Jane
Who Can Help?

Penguin Young Readers
An Imprint of Penguin Group (USA) Inc.

Contents

Chapter 1
Find Dick

Jane said, "I see you.

I see you, Sally.

I can find you.

I cannot find Dick.

Help me, Sally.

Help me find Dick."

Jane said, "Oh, Father.

I cannot find Dick.

And we cannot play.

Help me, Father.

Help me find Dick."

Father said, "Look, Jane.

Look, look, look.

You can find Dick."

Sally said, "Oh, oh.

I see Dick now.

Father and I see Dick.

We see funny Dick.

Look, Jane, look.

You can find Dick now."

Chapter 2
Who Can Help?

Dick said, "Mother, Mother.

Come here.

I want you.

Come and help me.

Oh, Jane.

Oh, Father.

Who can come?

Who can come and help me?"

Dick said, "Go away, Spot.

You cannot help me.

Oh, my.

Oh, my.

I want Mother.

Mother can help me.

Run, Spot, run.

Run and find Mother."

Dick said, "Oh, Spot.

Now I can come in.

You can help me.

Little Spot can help.

You can help me come in."

Chapter 3
See What I See

Dick said, "Look, Sally.

Look down here.

See what I see.

See my big cookie.

See me and my big cookie.

You can see Spot here.

Spot wants my big cookie."

"Oh, oh," said Sally.

"I see Tim and me.

And now I see Puff.

Puff is in here.

I see little Puff.

Puff and Tim and me."

Sally said, "Look, Jane.

Look down here.

You can see Jane in here."

Jane said, "Oh, oh, oh.

Who sees what I see?

It is something funny.

It is not Jane."

Chapter 4
Little Boat

Sally said, "See my boat.

I want my little boat.

I want my little boat in here."

Jane said, "Dick can get it.

Dick is big.

Dick can go and get it."

"Not now," said Dick.

"I cannot get it now."

Jane said, "Come, Sally.

Come and play.

Here is Tim."

"I want my boat," said Sally.

"Who can get it for me?

Is Father here?

Father can get it for me."

Sally said, "Oh, oh, oh.

Come here, Dick.

See what I see.

See my little blue boat now.

See who wants my boat.

My little blue boat.

See who wants it now."

Chapter 5
What Can Dick Make?

Jane said, "Look, Sally.

See what I can make.

It is big and yellow.

It is for Puff."

Sally said, "Look, Mother.

I can make something for Tim.

Jane can make something for Puff.

What can Dick make?"

Dick said, "I can make something.

Come and see what it is."

"Is it blue?" said Sally.

"Is it yellow?

Is it red?"

Dick said, "Oh, my.

It is red and yellow and blue.

Come and see what it is."

Jane said, "Look, Sally.

Dick can make something pretty.

See what Dick can make."

"I see it," said Sally.

"It is pretty.

What is it?"

Jane said, "Oh, Sally.

It is DICK."

Chapter 6
See It Go

Father said, "Look in here.

You can find something.

Something you want."

Dick said, "Look, Jane, look.

Red, yellow, and blue.

Yellow is for me.

Who wants red and blue?"

Jane said, "I want blue.

Red is for Sally."

Dick said, "Come, Sally.

Come and get something.

Red for you and blue for Jane."

Sally said, "Oh, Dick.

Pretty, pretty.

Make it big.

Make it big, big, big."

Jane said, "Run, Spot.

Run away, Puff.

See what I see.

Run, run, run."

"Now look," said Dick.

"See my boat.

See my boat go.

I can make it go away.

See it go.

Oh, see it go."

Chapter 7
Little Tim Can Help

Dick said, "Look, look.

Here we come.

We can help."

Jane said, "Run, Dick.

Run, run.

We can help."

"Look here," said Sally.

"One is for Dick.

One is for Jane.

And one is for Baby Sally."

"Look, Mother," said Sally.

"Here we come.

See little Tim.

Tim can help.

Tim can help Mother.

Oh, oh.

Tim is funny."